LEX LEADS THE WAY

The second story in **THE CAPABLES**® series

Created and Written by
Danny Jordan

Illustrated by
Agustina Perciante

Published by
The Capables LLC

Edited by
Alex Asher Sears

For Mom and Dad, thank you for always encouraging me to dream big and to look at the world in a different way.

-Danny

Library of Congress Control Number: 2022914393

ISBN 978-1-7364580-5-1 (hardback)
ISBN 978-1-7364580-6-8 (paperback)
ISBN 978-1-7364580-7-5 (ebook)

Printed and bound in the United States of America
Published in Los Angeles, California

First Edition, October 2022

Editor: Alex Asher Sears
Book design: Danny Jordan and Agustina Perciante
Publisher: The Capables LLC

Website: www.thecapables.com
Social Media: @thecapables

Lex was a kid with big, beautiful pictures in her head.

"You see the world differently" is what her mom always said.

Lex paced back and forth daydreaming, as she often did.

Her dad's words "I love the way your mind works" echoed in her head.

The morning was beautiful with a few perfectly puffy white clouds in view. The sky said hello in the most welcoming powder blue.

How are you feeling about the field trip?

Lex noticed the palms of her hands were sweaty...

...and her breath was getting shorter.

The joy she was feeling drifted away with the leaves.

Lex believed her mom, but she was still nervous.

Lex's best friend, Rae, came running over...

...and greeted her as she always did with a big smile and their secret handshake.

I'm sooo excited for today!

I can't wait to check out their solar system display...

...and the laser light show...

...oh, and I loooove the shooting-star slide...

Caught up in her own excitement, Rae didn't notice how quiet Lex was.

Is everything okay?

Yeah, it's just...

...ugh...

...you know my brain works differently.

I know!

We both have things that make us different.

I mean, you do remember what I did with the sun, and the rain, and the clouds, right?

Yeah...I know you say our differences make us super, but not everyone thinks that way.

Alright class...

...everyone is here. Time to get on the bus!

Rae wanted to encourage Lex but decided to give her friend some space.

SCHOOL BUS

I loooove this place!
Have you ever been here before?
Yeah, with my parents and Scotty a couple of times. It's pretty cool.

Hellooooo, class!
Welcome to the Discovery Dome!
I'm Yumi.

First stop, Operation: Space Exploration where stars, planets, and moons zoomed overhead and around them.

Next up was the Dino Dig where the group got to search for and uncover dinosaur fossils in a massive archaeological site.

You know, this is kind of my speciality, buddy.

Mom, I love you, but not now, please.

Alright, then maybe I can tell Max how much *you* know about dinosaur bones...

The next stop was the Speed Zone where Lex, Max, and Rae each got to build and race their very own model cars.

Lex was enjoying herself so much that the worries from earlier began to escape her mind.

Time for the next room, class!

The people on these walls dared BIG, explored BIG, and discovered BIG!

Take a few minutes to walk around and learn more about these BIG dreamers!

Lex was off on her own, looking at one of the portraits.

...ATHERINE

Slowly and quietly, she studied the words on the mural featuring mathematician Katherine Johnson.

...E JOHNSON

Ms. Johnson...

...was one of the first...

...African American women...

...to work as a NASA...

Hey! You're reading about one of my heroes: Katherine Johnson!

KATHERINE JOHNSON

Trying to read...

Take your time, baby girl. It's okay.

It was hard for Lex to slow down and take her time though. All of the other kids were bouncing around from one picture to another.

This is sooo fun! These people did such cooool things!

ALBERT EINSTEIN

Alright, kids, time to move on to the last activity for the day!

This way!

Yumi, who had been keeping an eye on Lex, walked over to her and her mom. They were the last three people in the room.

There's a lot of neat stuff to read in here, huh?

Yeah...My brain has difficulty recognizing words and letters, so it is a lot for me.

Believe it or not, I know the feeling.

I have dyslexia.

Really? Me too.

That makes three of us.

And we're not the only ones. Want to know something super cool?

Yep!

Can we get a hint, pleeease?

Not yet. Maybe try and look at the puzzle differently.

With the words "look at the puzzle differently," pictures began dancing around in Lex's head.

In her mind, the pieces began to float through the air—twisting, flipping, spinning, twirling—until the puzzle fit together perfectly.

Pretty cool, isn't it?

Uh-huh...I see how to solve the puzzle.

Me too.

Should I help, Mama?

It's your choice, but I think the world needs people whose minds work in different ways.

It's like Grammy says, **Different is SUPER!**

The pendant around Lex's neck was shining like the full moon in the night sky.

Empowerment was the key that unlocked Lex's superpower.

Lex took a deep breath and the puzzle pieces began to float in front of her again.

As the class moved back through the lobby towards the exit, Max ran up to Lex and Rae.

Lex!

Whoa, that was SO cool!

I couldn't even see the solution...

...and I can see *EVERYTHING* when I want to!

Did he just say...

Yes. Yes, he did.

They both smiled as they followed the group out into the fall sunshine.

That evening, Lex and her family had a backyard BBQ.

So, how was the field trip?

It was super... cool.

Yeah?

What made it so cool?

Well, I solved a very hard puzzle, and I learned all about some heroes who are just like Mom and me.

And now I know what I want to be when I grow up.

What's that?

A superhero-explorer-inventor-space scientist!

I love the way you think.

Because I'm capable of so many different things!

To be continued...

About the Author

Danny Jordan is an award-winning author and TV producer. When his daughter was born with an upper limb difference in 2018, he became an advocate for inclusion and accurate representation of disability in the media.

Danny's premiere book, *Rae's First Day: The First Story in The Capables Series*, received the Kirkus Star, the IBPA Benjamin Franklin Award, and was named one of the Best Books of 2021 by *Kirkus Reviews* magazine.

Outside of this thrilling literary adventure, Danny has produced and directed over 150 hours of primetime major network and cable television programming, along with co-hosting the #1 Christmas podcast in the world, *Christmas Countdown*.

Danny lives in Southern California with his family and their trusty pup, Sammy.

Follow Danny on Instagram @dannyjordan

About the Illustrator

Agustina Perciante is an Argentinian book illustrator, traditional painter, and sculptor based in Seattle, Washington.

To make art, Agustina relies on her heart. Conveying feelings through her art is the main focus of her work, and Agustina relies on a burst of emotion to create all of her pieces, inspiring other people to feel.

Follow Agustina on Instagram @percima.art

The Capables Advisory Board

Nicole Kelly, Kizzi Barazetti, Mika Jain, Larry Powell, Deborah Baker Jr., Amelia Baker Lauderdale, Rachael Owhin

Learn more about our advisory board's work and our mission at www.thecapables.com

A Note from the Author

We are committed to making each story in The Capables series accessible to all. One step we are taking with this book specifically is the use of a font called Dyslexie, which is a dyslexia-friendly font. Please visit dyslexiefont.com to learn more.

Additionally, as part of our mission to empower and educate, we are pleased to provide the following resources for anyone interested in learning more about dyslexia and the disability community:

The Dyslexia Foundation: dyslexiafoundation.org
Disability Visibility: disabilityvisibilityproject.com
Diversability: mydiversability.com

Acknowledgements

The second story in The Capables series was made possible through a successful Kickstarter campaign. We owe a very special thank you to the following people who supported us and made book two a reality:

Marilyn and Michael "Mom and Dad" Hollander, Andrew, Kelsey, and Wesley Hollander, Erin Hollander, Matthew Jordan, Aunt Pat, Mark Kennedy, Suzanne and Ken Epstein, Brian and Kathy Turner, Tracci and Lucy Falco, Uncle Mikey, Lucky Fin Project, Grandma and Grandpa Rachford, Grandma Bebe, Uncle Steve and Auntie Tania, Uncle Jim and Aunt Sue, Judy Rodriguez, Cameron Britton, Jason, Lisa, Landon, and Dawson Quartararo, The Love Family, Margy Rosenbluth, The Lane Family, Miranda Allen, Amelia Lauderdale, Alison, Bryan, Madelyn, and Arielle Friedman, The Simon Family, Catherine Ann Sisk, Valerie Mansourian, Dr. Lightdale-Miric, Aria Dang, Katie Pettit, Roberta Golden, Jim Head, Terry Wallace, Abigail Griebelbauer, Hayley Walters, The Costello Family, Paula and Jerry De Young, Ma'Ryia Mahome, The Patrick Family, Stacy Shepard, Erin Nagel, Michael German, Scott Gilbert and Mary Zastrow, John and Sharon Miller, Mady Villavicencio, Dana Cuneo, Carlee Clymer Powers, Christine Goodman Nuttall and Paul Nuttall, Heather Locke and the Hammersmith Team, Jim and Kathy Lowry, Skylar Franks, Lexis Serot and LittleWins.com, Kaelyn and Kelly McCamy Brown, and Diana MacLeod.

Additionally, the author would like to thank the following people for their time, support, and guidance throughout the creative process:

Lynn Jordan, Ryan J. Haddad, Rhett Reese, Chelsey Crisp, Jason Schneider, Brandi Passante, Kara Lindsay, Brandon Farbstein, Patrick Hinds, Dom Anders, Christine Di'Amore, Darrah Brustein, Rico Colindres, LJ Behlmann, Eric Petersen, Uniquely Me Foundation, Danielle Judovits, Christopher J. Hanke, Rosalie Mastaler, Kyle Mauch, Colleen D'Agostino, Reach Charity, Araksya Karapetyan, Stephanie Thomas, Danny Marin, Ben Cameron, JoJo Wright, IAMPOSSIBLE Foundation, Aussie Hands, Nicole Jordan, Kayley Wall, Jacob Balken, Anna Graves, Katie Kaye, Stephen Epstein, John Ewing, Nicole Silberstein, and Annie Watson.

CPSIA information can be obtained
at www.ICGtesting.com
Printed in the USA
BVHW012253111222
653967BV00004B/91